Tooth
Castleland

Terri Poirier

ISBN 979-8-89043-118-9 (paperback)
ISBN 979-8-89043-119-6 (digital)

Christian Faith Publishing
832 Park Avenue
Meadville, PA 16335
www.christianfaithpublishing.com

Printed in the United States of America

Dedicated to my Grandchildren
Lauren, Garrett, Sam, Lucas,
Carson, Mac and Brody

Did you ever wonder where
the tooth fairy takes the teeth
from under our pillows?

Some people say they
get thrown away,

CONSTRUCTION
SITE

THE
VILLAGE

others say they are put in tooth
piles by their sizes and shapes.

But I think, and you will agree,
that the tooth fairy takes our
teeth from under our pillow and
brings them to Tooth Fairy Land!

9

In Tooth Fairy Land, which
I might add, no one knows
where the teeth are collected,
and the tooth workers sort
teeth by size and shape.

The teeth are then moved to the
building area where the worker
tooth fairies design the castles
for the tooth fairy families.

These castles are all made from the teeth collected by the tooth fairies.

The teeth are all different sizes
and shapes, so the builders
can build the castles for each
of the family's needs.

**The teeth fit just right
for each castle.**

So take care of your teeth,
for your teeth could be the
home of your tooth fairy.

About the Author

Theresa E. Poirier likes to go by Terri.

Terri was born in Waterbury, Connecticut, and grew up with her parents, Armand and Agnes, in Oakville, Connecticut, also with her brother, Armand (Butch), and their dog, Skipper.

Terri went through grammar school in Oakville, and then went to junior high school, also in Oakville. She attended high school in Watertown, Connecticut, where she graduated. After graduation, she attended a business school in Waterbury, Connecticut.

She worked for Winchester Electronics, which later became Litton Industries in Oakville, Connecticut.

She later married David Poirier and resided in Watertown, Connecticut. Here they still live today. They have three children, Veronica, David, and Holly, and seven grandchildren. Her grandchildren gave her the idea for Tooth Castleland.

Terri worked in the Watertown Elementary School System for eleven years, six of which were in town elementary school libraries. From there, she went into industry where she worked as a purchasing manager but always had a desire to write children's books.

Terri always enjoyed working with young children, from coaching Little League Girl Softball to teaching Faith Formation at her church and starting an elementary school library volunteer program.

And so that is how Tooth Castleland got started. She would jot down questions from her grandchildren and keep them in a file until, one day, it was time.